This book belongs to:

THE ADVENTURES OF

LILY-MAY

HARE TODAY GONE TOMORROW

WRITTEN BY EMMA-JANE LEESON
ILLUSTRATED BY SALLY-ANN KELLY

BOOKS BY EMMA-JANE LEESON

THE ADVENTURES OF LILY-MAY SERIES:

FOUL FAERIES

HARE TODAY GONE TOMORROW

THE ADVENTURES OF JOHNNY MAGORY SERIES:

JOHNNY MAGORY IN THE MAGICAL WILD

JOHNNY MAGORY AND THE GAME OF ROUNDERS

JOHNNY MAGORY AND THE WILD WATER RACE

JOHNNY MAGORY AND THE FOREST FLEADH CHEOIL

JOHNNY MAGORY JOINS THE IRISH LEGENDS

JOHNNY MAGORY AND THE FARMYARD FÉASTA

JOHNNY MAGORY OÍCHE NOLLAG ADVENTURE

JOHNNY MAGORY SPRAOI BY THE SEA

THE ADVENTURES OF JOHNNY MAGORY COLLECTION

OTHER BOOKS:

ODE TO A TOMBOY

AISLING THE ADVENTUROUS CONKER

LITTLE L

WWW.JOHNNYMAGORY.COM

DOWNLOAD OUR APP 'JOHNNY MAGORY WORLD'

First published 2022 by The Johnny Magory Co. Ltd.

Ballynafagh, Prosperous, Naas, Co. Kildare, Ireland

ISBN 978-1-8382152-8-6

We're an independent Irish business who believe in keeping it local in all that we do. Here's how and where this little book was made:

Written & Designed by Emma-Jane Leeson, Co. Kildare

Edited by Geraldine Walsh, Co. Dublin

Illustrated by Sally-Ann Kelly, Co. Kildare

Printed by Anglo Printers, Co. Louth

We also believe in helping our planet. This book has been produced with sustainably sourced paper and free from plastic.

There's no need to continue reading this boring bit unless you're planning on getting up to no good (at which point we'd really love to hear from you to see if we can get in on the act too!)

For the ones who are so full of divilment...

EJ

Chapter 1

A legend shares a legend

"Ah, go on, Grandad. Tell me one more story," Lily-May begged her favourite grandparent. "Pleeease?"

"Alright, ye scallywag. One more," Grandad resigned, leaning back into his old brown armchair beside the blazing fire in the small, cluttered but cosy sitting room. It was nearly 8 o'clock on a Friday evening in mid-March. Lily-May and her Grandad were the only people in the Magory house. Her brother Johnny, Ma and Da, and their dog Ruairi were away watching the parish team play a hurling match. Lily-May loved when it was just her and Grandad at home. She could sit and listen to his stories all day, and oh how Grandad loved to tell stories.

"My favourite," Lily-May instructed with a smile, her long blonde hair bouncing on her fleecy navy pyjamas as she nodded her head enthusiastically.

"Alright then," he smiled and began. It didn't take much to persuade him. This was one of his favourite legends too.

"Long, long ago in Ireland when the country was covered in thick forests where wolves, bears and boars roamed, and the men were strong and as big as giants, there lived a mighty warrior named Oísin.

"Oísin was the son of Fionn MacCumhaill and his love Sadhbh. Now Sadhbh, I've told you before, was cursed by an evil olde sod. A dreadful druid named Fear Doirich, which means 'Dark Man.' He turned poor Sadhbh into a deer again after Oísin was born and..."

"Wait," Lily-May interrupted, "tell me about Sadhbh again. The deer part."

"You and your shapeshifters," Grandad joked. "Alright, so. Sadhbh was a looker, a true Irish beauty and the daughter of the great king, Bodb Dearg. Fear Doirich, the dodgy druid, asked Sadhbh to marry him, and she was having none of it. No way, José!

"This obviously didn't float too well with the druid, so he cursed poor Sadhbh, turning her into a doe. You know the song?" Grandad asked, clearing his throat and starting to sing. "Doe a deer, a female deer, ray a drop of golden sun, me..."

"Yes, Grandad," Lily-May laughed as she sang with him, "a name I call myself! Far a long, long way to run!"

Grandad smiled. Eager to hear more, she coaxed him on, "I know what a doe is. Tell me more about Sadhbh."

Grandad chuckled. "Well, poor Sadhbh was so sad being a deer. She wandered here and wandered there until eventually, one day, Fionn MacCumhail's giant hounds, Bran and Sceólan, spotted her. They knew she was a human because, da, da, daaaaa," he announced, standing up for effect, "those hounds were once human too. But don't even go there tonight, Miss Magory. That's one for another night!" he hastily stated before moving on quickly not to give her the chance of interrupting again.

"So, when they brought Sadhbh back to Oísin, she turned back into her beautiful human self, and of course, herself and Mister MacCumhaill fell madly in love and got married." Grandad hummed the tune of *'Here comes the bride'* before continuing.

"Shortly after, the gorgeous babogue Oísin arrived. Everyone was delighted until one day, Fionn had to go to war to defend Ireland."

Lily-May resembled a statue sitting cross-legged on the floor at Grandad's feet. The fire crackled and illuminated her rosy cheeks.

"Well, that dodgy druid Fear Doirich acted quickly to trick poor Sadhbh. He turned her into a deer again, and alas, no matter how far and wide he hunted, Fionn never saw his gorgeous wife again," Grandad said with a sad, heavy sigh.

"Wow," Lily-May said in amazement. "Do you think Grandad that someone could turn someone else into a deer nowadays? I mean, does the magic still exist?" she asked, wide-eyed.

With a chuckle and a twinkle in his eye, Grandad said, "I've told you before child. There's magic everywhere, especially in the woods. You just need to find it. Anyways, where was I?"

"We're just at the start of my favourite story about Oísin, Grandad," Lily-May exclaimed, rolling her eyes playfully at his forgetfulness, "Ye haven't even got to him yet!"

"Right throw another sod of turf on the fire there, young one, and I'll keep going," he said as he propped himself up on his old chair, preparing for the punchline in his performance.

"So, Oísin, ah yes Oísin. He was out hunting one day for his supper. There were no supermarkets in those days, let me tell ye. Ye had to hunt your supper, or ye simply didn't eat.

"Anyways, he spotted a big, beautiful hare galloping majestically through the long grass in an open glade in the forest. Without missing a beat, he aimed and threw his long, sharp, wooden spear."

With this, Grandad stood up out of his chair and re-enacted the throw like an Olympic champion stretching his arms out wide and swinging around, causing the flames on the fire to flicker as his quick movements fired up a breeze.

"Slap," he shouted as he clapped his strong, weathered hands sharply together, making Lily-May jump in fright.

"His spear hit the hare, knocking it over with force. Now, Oísin was quite chuffed with himself, although he never really missed in fairness. He tossed his long blonde hair over his shoulder and began to stride across to his supper," Grandad said, imitating the proud Oísin, as he stood out of his chair and took large strides on the spot of the worn carpet. Just as Oísin would have, he held his head up high. His tweed paddy-cap fell over his eyes as the stride knocked it off balance. Grandad jerked it back onto his head with a firm finger and a grunt.

"When suddenly," Grandad sprung back into action, "up sprang the hare. It started to run across the glade and back into the forest. The hare was clearly injured on its hind leg. Blood dripping down. Limping on it. The works. So Oísin took chase after the hare as it darted into the thick trees. Running through ferns and bracken, then briars and nettles, he never flinched once. That's how hardy he was, you see.

He eventually stopped when he came to a cliff face, a hundred feet high." Grandad stood bolt upright and tilted his head back towards the ceiling as if he was standing at the bottom of the one-hundred-foot cliff.

"He saw the hare run straight at it, so he bent down and pulled back the thorns in front of him with his bare hands," Grandad smiled for a moment at Lily-May as she sat cross-legged on the floor looking up at his great height. The flames from the fire flickered in her eyes as he said, "Hardy man, remember." He knelt and stretched out his arms, pretending to pull at the vines before dusting down his empty hands on his creased trousers and nestling back into the armchair.

"In the rock," he continued, "Oísin found a wooden door with big black cast-iron hinges and a wooden doorknob carved with the head of a hare on it. He turned the handle and slowly pushed the door.

"Creeaaaakkkk," Grandad groaned as he stretched his strong hands out to push an imaginary door.

Lily-May sat as still as a statue on the floor enchanted, her eyes as wide as saucers. The knuckles on her right hand were white from her grip on her fleecy pyjama top, but she did not notice.

"A great big stair lay in front of him going down, down, down into the deep dark Earth," Grandad almost whispered as though to echo the cavernous staircase he imagined.

"Now, a normal man would have turned around at this point, but not Oísin. No, he was as brave as a mad bull, so down he went, spear in hand. Step by step, lower and lower, down and down until thud. Oísin finally reached the last step,"

Grandad's hands flew about him as he slowly swung them, giving a sense of enormous space.

"In front of his very eyes was a huge room with torches of fire lighting on the wall and a huge throne in the centre. When his eyes adjusted to the light, he saw a beautiful woman sitting on the throne crying. Her leg was bleeding."

Even though Lily-May had heard this story a hundred times, she still gasped when Grandad delivered his dramatic punchline.

"The beautiful, mysterious woman told Oísin that the hares of Ireland were all shapeshifters who spent their lives between the body of a human and the body of hare. Enchanted with magic, they helped the land grow in abundance, ensuring its longevity and constant rebirth with each new moon," Grandad said in a serious, awestruck tone. His small, wrinkled dark-brown eyes seemed to stare off into the distance with a look of longing for a moment.

"Now, Oísin couldn't believe it. Sure, of course, he had heard stories like this before, but it was one of those things that he needed to see to believe. The blood dripping from the leg of the mysterious woman was all it took for his mind to be made up. Well, the blood and the stern telling off he got from the magical lady.

"Three other hares appeared from behind the woman's throne, two girls and a boy that he at once knew were her children. Their deep brown eyes pierced Oísin's very soul as he dropped his head in sorrow and bent down on one knee, giving his word that he was a changed man.

"And so, from that day onwards, Oísin nor any of the members of the great Na Fianna army ever ate a hare again. Sin é," he finished triumphantly, taking a little bow before he sat back down into his chair and revelled at his own performance.

Hopping up and down with excitement, Lily-May's hands began to sting with her ferocious applause. Her imagination was running wild. Grandad Magory really was one of the best storytellers in Ireland. Everyone said it.

"Wow, Grandad, it just never gets old. What a story. Do hares still shapeshift? Oh, I hope they do, can you just imagine," Lily-May said, her gaze drifting off to the rooftops as she imagined chasing the hares in the woods.

"Young one, I've told ya before, there's still magic there. Ye just need to know where to look." He winked at Lily-May as he stood to stretch his slim and ageing but strong body.

"Now, after all that talk of supper, I'm starving!" he exclaimed. "Come 'ere till I tell ya, would ye eat a bit of cold cabbage if I heated it up for ya?" he said to Lily-May with a serious look, then burst into a laugh at his granddaughter's puzzled expression at his old joke.

Grandad clicked the kettle on and toasted slices of soda bread. Lily-May sat at the table, running her finger along the Celtic pattern decorating the tablecloth. Following each swirl and curve, she thought deeply about Oísin and the hares. And, of course, the magic.

The almost full moon shone through the window, highlighting the frost growing on it. Eating around the crust of the soda bread, Lily-May suddenly had an idea. A plan! Tomorrow, she thought to her herself, she would find out the truth about shapeshifters.

Once and for all.

Chapter 2
Into the Magical Wild

Lily-May sleepily rubbed her eyes as she threw back the covers to grab her dressing gown and pulled it up around her shoulders. The frost on the windowpane looked like a thick jungle of ferns in the undergrowth of the forest, she thought as she stepped into her slippers. Intending to make her way to the kitchen for breakfast, she remembered her plan with a surge of enthusiasm. Her brain clicked into gear.

She found it nearly impossible to sleep the night before with the excitement. She quickly pulled out thick black leggings, a long-sleeved blue top and a fleecy red jumper from her drawers.

She dug around for the thickest pair of long socks she could find before hopping from one foot to the other as she pulled on her trousers. In her haste, her head momentarily got stuck in the arm of her jumper!

Her attempt at making the bed wasn't perfect with the stripey yellow duvet crooked, but it would do. Her goldfish, Zig and Zag, demanded their breakfast as a plop of water loudly splashed from the tank onto the wooden floor.

"I wasn't going to forget you guys," Lily-May smiled as she sprinkled the multicoloured flakes on the top of the clear water. "Now, I've really gotta run!"

Johnny, her big brother, was coming out of the bathroom yawning and rubbing his eyes. His normally chaotic black hair was messier than usual, standing on end like he had been electrocuted! They almost collided as Lily-May raced for the top of the stairs.

"Where are you going in such a hurry?" he asked with a yawn.

"Into the Magical Wild to see Finn Hare," she answered as she began to step down the stairs. "I need to talk to him about something. Are you coming?"

"Nah, not now. I've training this morning. Ruairi's coming to the pitch with me too," he answered with a hint of disappointment in his voice. Finn Hare was Johnny's best friend in the Magical Wild, and he still loved to go through the secret rabbit hole more than anything else in the world.

"Are you sure you're alright on your own?" Johnny asked his sister.

"Eh, yes. Why wouldn't I be?" she snapped back, pausing, and turning back to her brother, rolling her eyes as she reached the bottom of the stairs and made her way to the kitchen.

Johnny shrugged and sleepily made his way towards his bedroom. He wondered if he could get an extra few minutes in bed before Ma called him to get ready.

"You're dressed bright and early," Ma greeted Lily-May as she hurriedly made her way to get a bowl of the warm porridge already cooked on the stove.

"Morning Mammy," Lily-May smiled and stopped to give her Ma a quick hug. "Yep, I'm going exploring."

She began shovelling spoonful after spoonful of porridge into her mouth, too excited to sit down.

"Great to hear," Grandad agreed, lifting his head from behind a giant newspaper at the kitchen table.

"I've to bring your brother to the pitch for training shortly," Ma said, "and your father and Grandad need to fix up the lawnmower out in the shed today.

Thankfully spring is on the way at last," Ma smiled. She loved the warmer half of the year. "Will you be ok exploring on your own?"

"Why does everyone keep asking me that?" Lily-May said through pinched lips and her hands on her hips. "Of course, I'll be ok. I'm eight years old, aren't I?"

"Ah, when I was your age child, sure we were practically reared," Grandad interjected. "Working on the farm or in the bogs, cooking, cleaning, drinking porter." He joked with a grin and a wink. He loved to have a pint of porter in the pub and tell stories to his friends. "Sure, what harm can a clever young cailín like you get up to on your own?"

"Less of it, Grandad," Ma warned with a smirk as she reached across the table and topped up his cup of tea with a hot drop from the pot.

Lily-May gobbled her porridge with honey in record time, raced back up the stairs to brush her teeth, said 'goodbye' to her goldfish and leapt back down the stairs towards the backdoor.

She threw on her puffy mustard coat, zipping it right up to the top to keep the chill out. Then, pulling on her grey woolly hat over her curly brown mop, Lily-May tested her trusty torch that sat in the middle of her favourite hat. It worked, nice and bright. On went her multicoloured striped wellies while she fumbled around for her gloves.

Ma dropped a flask of strong, hot tea into her backpack along with some soda bread and raspberry jam they made last autumn from the berries that grew in the hedges. She wrapped them in a tissue and popped in a bright red apple too.

"Thanks Ma," Lily-May smiled as she ran over to hug her. "See you later. Love you."

"Love you too, mó stór. Don't be late back now. The evenings are still dark," Ma cautioned.

"I know," Lily-May answered as she opened the back door and the chilly air hit her. "Oh, it's Baltic!" she gasped but jumped out over the step and shouted, "K bye!"

The grass crunched under her feet as she ran across the lawn towards the large rabbit hole that lay under the hedge surrounding their garden. The frost left a perfect trail of her movements, holding onto each footprint for as long as it could before the sun warmed up.

She ducked down without hesitation and, on her hands and knees, began crawling into the familiar dark, tight tunnel that was a passage from one world to another.

The world it led into was not like the one she was leaving. This was a world where Mother Nature and her creatures communicated with the children. Foxes, badgers, and hawks were not merely beautiful wildlife that you might catch a glimpse of in the distance if you were lucky. In this world, they were friends, companions, and guardians to the children.

And the magic didn't stop at the wildlife. Even the trees spoke softly and whispered amongst themselves. Some were even known to sing silly, happy songs.

This was the world Johnny had discovered thanks to their dog Ruairi, who wasn't any ordinary canine! As cute, floppy and fluffy as he was in the everyday world, Ruairi was king of the Magical Wild; noble, astute and fiercely respected by every creature. Well, most of them, but that's another story!

As Lily-May crawled further into the tunnel, the noises of her world, like the traffic on the nearby road, a mobile phone ringing in the pocket of someone out walking, and the hum of electricity cables began to fade. The further she went, the quieter it became until she finally emerged the other side to be immersed in a cocoon of perfect calm.

The frost touched everything in sight, reminding Lily-May of Narnia. There was not a sound to be heard in this frozen world. Pure bliss.

Lily-May drew a deep inhale, filling her lungs with the crystal-clear air. Exhaling, she watched the swirls and shapes her frosty breath made against the backdrop of the Magical Wild. The mystical shapes reminded her of her mission.

In an instant, she was on her feet, galloping gleefully through the forest that lay ahead of her. The rhythmic crunching of frost under her feet and her warm steamy breath moved with her. She knew the path so well. She didn't even have to look down. She knew she would be approaching the Golden River, where Master

Willow would be waiting patiently to bring her across. She followed the path as it sharply turned right around a mighty Scots Pine tree but suddenly... Whack!

Chapter 3
A little guidance

Lily-May slipped on the icy path as her foot went from underneath her. She fell heavily onto the right side of her body with a loud thud as she hit the ground with force.

"Owww!" she cried out in both pain and shock, her cry echoing through the frozen forest.

As she gently pulled herself to her feet, a familiar voice called, "Are you ok, my dear?"

It was Mae Robin who was one of her favourite creatures in the Magical Wild. A true dear friend to her, Johnny, and Ruairi.

"I came as soon as I heard you shout," she flustered. "Oh, did you slip, you poor little mite? Are you hurt? Is anything broken? Do I need to get Joseph Stag to help?"

"I'm ok, Mae, honest," Lily-May said, forcing out a smile and reassuring her little friend. "I just banged my leg, that's all. Another little bruise to add to the collection, no doubt."

"Are you sure?" Mae Robin asked again, worry clear in her voice.

"Yes, promise," Lily-May smiled. "Sorry for disturbing you, Mae. You're probably busy, and the last thing you need is to be here looking over me."

"Not at all, dear. Sure, the food is well frozen over for another few hours yet, I'm glad of something to keep me moving, keep me warm," Mae Robin answered with a shiver, fluffing up her beautiful red breast. "What has you here alone today anyways? We weren't expecting Ruairi back until nightfall?"

"Yeah, I came alone this morning," Lily-May answered before spotting an opportunity. "Mae, what do you know about the hares shapeshifting?"

"Oh, well," Mae answered, a little taken aback as she hadn't been expecting a question like that. "Well, what do *you* know?" she asked hesitantly.

Lily-May's heart began to beat quicker with excitement as she realised Mae Robin did know something after all as she didn't laugh at her inquisitive question.

"Grandad reckons that the magic is still alive, Mae," said Lily-May as the pair walked along the Golden River towards Master Willow. "That it can still be done? Is that true?"

"That Grandad of yours. How is he doing, dear? Tell him I was asking, won't you," Mae chirped happily.

"Of course, Mae, but what do you know?" Lily-May asked with excitement and slight agitation clear in her voice.

"Well, dear, I'm not too familiar with the hare's practices or traditions, so perhaps I am not the best to be getting information from." Noticing the disappointment in Lily-May's face, she said, "but all I do know is that something magic happens each full moon."

Lily-May's heart skipped a beat. Mae had just confirmed something happened, and tonight was the full moon. The Worm Moon. And Ma said it was very special for it to fall on the Spring Equinox this year, so that had to mean something too.

Arriving at the edge of the Golden River, Lily-May noticed the water was frozen solid like a giant ice rink. Mae Robin flew upwards to the top of the giant willow tree on the banks. Tapping her right wing gently on the warm brown bark of the trunk, she chirped a bright, cheery song waking up the sleeping tree.

A booming, cheerful voice could be heard echoing through the forest. It was that of Master Willow, the enchanted tree that helped the children cross over the Golden River each time they visited.

"Oh, how great it is to see thee,

But today, you need not sit on me.

Hold out your hand, grab a branch, have some faith,

This frozen river and frozen tree would love for you to skate!"

The tree happily sang as it delicately moved a small branch like a hand towards Lily-May, bending into a little hook at the end which enabled her to hold onto it.

Mae Robin laughed at Master Willow and Lily-May as theygiggled and skated their way across the frozen river.

"Dear, I'm going to fly back quickly to check the fledglings. I'll catch up with you later, ok?" she chirped.

"No probs, Mae. Thanks a mil for keeping me company," Lily-May answered as she glided along, led by Master Willows branch to the other side of the river.

Once she was safely on the other bank, she turned and gave a little curtsy to Master Willow, thanking him for his help in crossing.

The face in the huge tree trunk gave a warm smile, then simply disappeared as the branches resumed their normal shape and stiffened.

Lily-May picked up a quick trot again to keep warm. She was buzzing with excitement, her mind awash with ideas. She could see a familiar shape on the path ahead and sped up to reach it quicker.

"Hey, Sean-Óg," she called out to the beautiful red fox who was busy sniffing the base of the trees on the path.

"Oh, hey, Lily-May," the fox answered, turning around to face her with a smile. Sean-Óg was a young fox, no longer a cub but not quite an adult yet. Lily-May and Johnny viewed him as a teenager. He was still full of childhood fun, although extremely clever. The thing Lily-May and Johnny loved the most about Sean-Óg was his curiosity. It was contagious. He had to find out as much as he possibly could about everything he possibly could find out about! It had led to more than a few fantastic adventures last summer with the trio.

"What are you doing?" Lily-May asked.

"Trying to figure out who was along this path early this morning," he answered, his mind elsewhere. "It's a scent I don't fully recognise, although it does seem vaguely familiar."

"Oh," said Lily-May, her interest also peaked.

"What are you doing on your own?" Sean-Óg asked. "Are you ok out here on your own?"

"Yes!" Lily-May answered with annoyance in her voice at being asked by everyone she had met so far today. "I'm here to try and discover something," she said, purposely trailing off as she knew this would grab Sean-Óg's attention.

He sidled up beside Lily-May, curling his bushy tail around her as he circled her, eager to know what she was talking about. With his deep golden amber eyes narrowed, he held her gaze without blinking. She certainly had his attention now.

"What do you know about the hares being shapeshifters?" she blurted out in haste while she carefully watched his every move in response.

A grin spread across the fox's face as he responded, "not enough... yet. Tell me, what do *you* know?"

Lily-May smiled, knowing she had picked up a worthy sidekick for her adventure.

"Come on," she gestured as she began to run again. "I'll tell you what I know on the way."

And the two of them took off, running through the thick frozen forest.

Chapter 4

What's the story?

Johnny was making short work of Grandads steaming hot vegetable soup in the kitchen. He was ravenous after training.

"Where's Lily-May?" Johnny asked Grandad as he dunked some tasty homemade soda bread into his bowl.

"Exploring," Grandad answered, wiggling his long wrinkly fingers in front of his face like a magician about to cast a vanishing spell.

"What were you telling her stories about last night?" Johnny asked, longing clear in his voice. He loved his Grandad's stories too.

"Oh, just the usual story," he paused for a moment, "about a bold boy named Johnny Magory!" Grandad quipped and laughed at his little rhyme.

"Grandad," Johnny said, rolling his eyes. "Seriously, which one did you tell her?"

"Right, I'll tell you a story then, Johnny Magory," Grandad began as he took a seat opposite Johnny at the kitchen table with a serious look. "Will I start?" he continued before he paused and answered his own question, "It was just a fart!" And with that, he erupted, laughing at his own joke!

"Grandad!" Johnny cried out, laughing at his Grandad. "You're such a messer!"

When Grandad managed to gather himself together, he told Johnny about the strength and courage of Oísin and how he followed the injured hare to the underground cave.

"So, let me guess," Johnny said when his grandad had finished the tale through a mouthful of soup and brown bread, "Lily-May has gone to find out if it's true?"

"Do ye reckon?" Grandad said with a smile and shrug.

Johnny cleaned up after his lunch before he changed into warmer clothes. There was no way he was letting his sister have this adventure on her own. He wanted in on the secret the same way she did.

He made for the backdoor after he pulled on his wellies and coat. Ruairi by his side, of course.

"Fill me in when you return," Grandad said with a wink as he made his way back down to the shed to help Daddy with the lawnmower.

"And don't be gone all day Johnny," Ma shouted after him, but it was too late. He and Ruairi had already disappeared inside the rabbit hole.

Chapter 5
Telling tails

"So, that's basically what I know so far," Lily-May finished, slightly out of breath as she and Sean-Óg ran towards the opening at the edge of the forest.

"And let me guess, Finn Hare is where we're running to?" Sean-Óg asked with a knowing smile.

"Yep," Lily-May quickly answered, "straight to Finn, then hopefully he can let us know the truth once and for all. So come on, I've told you everything I know. Your turn to spill the beans."

As they reached the last of the tall alder trees that surrounded the forest, the morning sun had finally begun to send some heat towards the frozen earth. Beyond the forest lay an open glade, mainly flat and covered in grass and bracken during the summer. The odd hawthorn tree and cluster of shrubs dotted throughout the opening. On the other side of the clearing lay the beautiful Bullrush Lake. Beyond that again rose the wild hills and mountains.

The birds had started to land on the ground in the hope of catching worms as the earth thawed. The faintest smell of the sweet coconut-like fragrance of the early bright yellow gorse flowers that shimmered in the sun and frost wafted through the air.

"Well, as much of a famous storyteller that Paddy Magory is with the humans, my grandfather, Seán Sionnach, is just as renowned here," Sean-Óg began, "and there have been a few occasions when he mentioned the hares and the full moons."

The corners of Lily-May's mouth curled up slightly as she clenched her teeth. Her fingers clenched inside her coat pocket. She knew she was about to uncover another clue in her quest.

Out of the corner of her eye, she noticed an elegant slink-like movement in the darkness of the trees and slowed to a walk. Sean-Óg followed his gait and stopped running, raising his cold black nose into the air and sniffing the scent.

"Oísin! Fiadh!" she yelled as her eyes adjusted to see two beautiful young deer emerge from the darkness into the light of the grassy meadow where she and Sean-Óg now stood.

The animals gracefully made their way across the frozen grass to greet their human and fox friend.

"What has you here?" Fiadh Fawn asked in her well-spoken voice, her long dark eyelashes moving up and down elegantly as she spoke, making her huge brown eyes twinkle in the sun.

"And where's Johnny?" Oísin Fawn questioned in his similar regal tone, although he seemed more interested in unearthing some frozen grass from under his powerful hoof.

"I'm here on a mission," Lily-May

began, “alone. Well, not entirely alone. Sean-Óg is helping me.”

“Oh, what kind of mission?” Fiadh asked curiously, lowering her pretty head down a few inches and dropping her usually cool manner for a more friendly, inquisitive tone.

Fiadh and Oísin were members of the red deer herd. They had been best friends since they were born less than two years ago. Both were as beautiful and graceful as each other, although they weren't interested in mischief, unlike the smaller mammals in the wild. Instead, the deer’s tended to hold a more regal, serious position in society.

They were a little different to the rest of the herd, though. They enjoyed having adventures with Johnny and Lily-May, even if the rest of the herd their age turned their noses up at it a little.

“Lily-May wants to find out if the hares shapeshift for real,” Sean-Óg answered, “and truth be told, so do I.” He grinned at his friends.

"Ohhh, I think they do, Lily-May," Fiadh squealed excitedly. "My father, the boring old fart, always gives out about the racket they make during the full moon."

"Yes, indeed," Oísin continued, "same here. Interfering old witch women' is what my mother calls them."

"Witch women?!" Lily-May exclaimed, her eyes the size of saucers with intrigue.

"Yes indeed. Father says the same," Fiadh agreed with Oísin.

"And that kind of ties in with what my Grandad says in his stories," Sean-Óg continued, the excitement almost tangible in his voice, "but instead of witch women, he calls them Sidhe hares. Which I suppose is similar but backwards, depending on what angle you look at it from," he said,

"Sidhe ?" Lily-May asked.

Fiadh rolled her eyes as Sean-Óg was so deep in thought that he didn't hear Lily-May.

"Another name for the fae, although typically linked back far beyond the fairies we know today," Fiadh informed her.

"Around the time of the Tuatha de Deannan and the ancient goddesses," Oísin continued.

"Basic first-year-of-life history lessons, you know," Fiadh said with a flick of her beautiful head.

Lily-May barely caught the sarcastic 'tut' that came from her lips at the thought of everyone finding this out in the first year of their life history lessons. As if!

"Of course," she said aloud, not wanting to look foolish, although, in truth, she had little idea of what they were talking about. She quickly continued so nobody would question her on it.

"So, it's true then?" her voice was barely able to contain the excitement. "The hares are actually shapeshifters?"

Before getting a definite answer, a loud crash interrupted their conversation, followed by the creaking crack of smashing ice and a shrill scream.

"Heeeellllllpppppppppp!"

Chapter 6
The clash of fire and ice

On the other side of the glade, a hare was fighting for its life against the freezing waters of Bullrush Lake. A thin spot of ice cracked beneath his sturdy weight, quickly slipping him under the icy water.

The four friends watched in horror from across the glade where they stood. They ran as fast as they could to help but knew they were too far away to get there in time.

Their insides tight with anxiety, they watched on in horror as they ran, noticing the splashing becoming smaller and the voice becoming quieter. Even if they got there quicker, how could they help without putting themselves in danger? All four of them, Lily-May, Sean-Óg, Fiadh and Oísin, were heavier than a hare was. The ice would give way under them too.

They didn't stop though. They kept sprinting as fast as their legs could carry them towards the lake.

The cries for help slowly faded out and then stopped. They were still half the glade away.

"Oh no," sobbed Lily-May through the tears that ran down her cheek. "Oh no, please no," but still she ran.

Suddenly there was a shrill screech overhead. So loud and clear through the still freezing air, it frightened the four friends.

"Pádraig!" Lily-May cried out in hope as she saw her friend Pádraig Buzzard soar then dive from the sky, nose-first, towards where the hare had fallen in.

The speed at which he did this was hard for Lily-May's eyes to follow, but within a split second, the buzzard was flying back upwards again, a sleek, lifeless brown hare dangling lifelessly from its claws.

The onlooker's hearts sank as they realised who the hare was.

Finn.

Pádraig flew towards the four with Finn tight in his clays. It was clear he wasn't used to carrying this weight as he laboured with the uneven flapping of his usually graceful wings.

In a matter of moments, he was in front of the group and gently dropped Finn's limp body onto a tuff of frozen grass.

"Help him," he yelled in fear to the others. "Help him."

"It's too late," Fiadh answered, her head lowered.

"No, it's not," Lily-May screamed. "It's never too late. Quick, Sean-Óg gather up the longest twigs and rushes you can find," she instructed the fox.

"Pádraig, go and get his family as fast as you can. Explain what's happened. Fiadh, you look for the good fae in the woods. Tell them we need their help." She pointed towards the trees as Fiadh nodded and ran.

"And Oísin," she said finally, "quickly. Find Ruairi and my brother."

Oísin also nodded and took off at the fastest gallop she had ever seen.

Lily-May pulled off her bag pack and coat. She wrapped it around the lifeless body of Finn. She vigorously began rubbing his body all over, her hands working as quickly as possible.

"Finn! Finn! Don't leave us, Finn. Come on, Finn, stay with us," she cried.

Sean-Óg returned with the twigs and rushes just as Fiadh came into sight from the woods. Two tiny glowing fairies named Cillian and Caoimhe sat on her back as she galloped towards the trio.

"What can we do, Lily-May?" cried Cillian, one of the beautiful little fae, when they were just a few strides away.

"Light these twigs and make a fire," Lily-May instructed as she kept rubbing and crying out to Finn.

The two fairies took out their wands and muttered an incantation under their breaths. Within moments there was a blazing fire beside them. The heat of it visibly melted the frost from the grass around it and cast a warm glow across Lily-May's face as she sat crossed legged with Finn hare in her mustard coat on her lap.

"Take the flask from my backpack," she directed the second tiny fae Caoimhe, nodding her head towards her bag.

The two fairies worked together to unzip Lily-May's bag and carry over the black flask.

"Push that silver button on the top and try to pour some of the tea into his mouth," Lily-May continued with her instructions, all the while rubbing Finn's body wrapped in her coat in an attempt to heat it up.

The fairies did just as they were told, and drops of warm tea drizzled over Finn's brown lips.

"What now?" Fiadh asked, terror and anxiety in her normally even voice.

"Pray," Sean-Óg said as he rushed off to find more twigs.

Chapter 7
Bad news travels fast

"So, I got my boot right under the ball Mae, and kicked with all my might," Johnny shouted with excitement as he enthusiastically re-enacted that morning's training session for Mae Robin. At the same time, he and Ruairi waited for Master Willow to lower his branches for them to cross the Golden River.

The ice was beginning to melt, so Ruairi and Johnny could not skate across as Lily-May had earlier.

"Well done, Johnny," Mae Robin chirped in delight and clapped her wings.

Johnny stood up, chest out, shoulder back, head high, clearly delighted with his sporting efforts. Ruairi sat beside him and smiled while he waited patiently for the branch to drop beside them.

A cheerful loud voice began to bellow in song from above them.

"Oh, hop onboard my arm,

I won't do you any harm.

As you float across the air,

Your destination will be right there!"

Johnny and Ruairi chuckled together at Master Willows song. They thanked him as they stepped down from their branch on the far side of the Golden River.

"So, what do you guys know about the hares shapeshifting?" Johnny asked Ruairi and Mae Robin as they moved along through the deep thawing forest. "Is Grandad pulling Lily-May's leg, or is there something to it?"

"Is it time to let the *hare* out of the bag, Ruairi?" Mae Robin smirked at Ruairi as she fluttered along above the running pair.

"*Hare*ful now, Mae, we don't want to give too much away," Ruairi joked back.

Both of them laughed at their jokes.

"Har, har, har," Johnny said sarcastically. "Very funny."

"Don't you mean *hare, hare, hare*?" Ruairi answered and burst out laughing.

"Seriously," Johnny said, coming to an abrupt stop, crossing his arms and staring at his friends with pleading brown eyes.

"Alright, boy," Ruairi answered, although he was still chuckling at his bad jokes. "I know a lot about it, as you can imagine, but it's not something that's freely spoken about out here. The hares like to keep a low profile about that part of their lives. You know, an *ear* to the ground!"

Johnny decided to ignore Ruairi's terrible joke, but he was intrigued. He hadn't thought it was possible. The sensible part of his brain assumed Grandad was telling an old yarn, winding Lily-May and him up. Now he was excited. This was a pretty amazing thing, and he knew why Lily-May was so fascinated.

He was about to tell Ruairi he wouldn't breathe a word to anyone other than Lily-May when suddenly the sound of galloping hooves broke his thoughts. The furious pace was getting louder and closer. Johnny,

Ruairi, and Mae straightened their backs and turned towards the sound. Ruairi pushed forward in front of Johnny as Mae fluttered above his head.

Ruairi knew it wasn't safe for any animal to race at such a volatile speed on such a frosty morning with the treacherous icy ground. Who would be in such a hurry, he nervously wondered?

Around the corner, about twenty metres in front of them, a clearly panicked Oísin Fawn came into view, nostrils flaring, panting heavily, his legs almost a blur at the speed they were moving.

"Oísin! Stop!" Ruairi shouted as he stood onto his back legs and held his paws out in front of him.

Oísin skidded, leaning back on his hind legs with his front legs outstretched in front of him as he tried to come to a halt. He was only a metre away from the trio when he finally stopped, narrowly missing a collision. Steam emerged into the freezing air from his body while his panting breath rose above his face.

"Ruairi," he cried, trying to catch his breath, "quickly! Finn Hare has fallen into the frozen lake. I think he's dead."

They gasped in unison as their faces dropped and tight knots formed in their bellies.

"Lily-May has him on this side of the lake, hurry," he said before collapsing from exhaustion on the side of the path.

Without a word, Johnny, Ruairi, and Mae raced towards the glade, their minds a blur with anxiety and terror. Mae's tiny wings hummed as they quickly fluttered. Ruairi's powerful paws pounded off the frozen earth in a gallop. Johnny straightened his hands to help him cut through the air quicker. They moved faster than they ever went in their lives. Nobody spoke as the glistening frozen trees blurred past.

Ruairi was the first to spot the smoke and flames across the other side of the clearing as they emerged from the forest. He pushed his body even harder, speeding up. He didn't know what he would do when he got there. He didn't know what he'd find. A

million thoughts rushed through his head. Ruairi was the king in this world. The ruler of every creature. He knew every family. He was a loyal and faithful ruler. The safety and wellbeing of each creature was the only thing that mattered to him.

As he sped towards his friends, Ruairi's paws hit the cold ground with ferocious force. He was particularly fond of Finn Hare, and he knew that he and Johnny were best friends. Finn's cleverness and boldness was the perfect match for Johnny's.

He thought of Finn's mother, Eostre, and sisters Arleigh and Amaris. His heart saddened even further. He pushed his body to move faster.

Johnny had tears in his eyes, his mind a blur. He loved Finn. This couldn't be true. He could see the fire ahead and smell the burning branches in the smoke that floated towards them. Lily-May, Fiadh Fawn, Pádraig Buzzard, Sean-Óg Fox and three hares sat around it with their heads lowered.

As he got closer, he could see Lily-May holding something on her lap.

“We’re here,” Ruairi shouted out when they were within ears reach.

The group around the fire lifted their lowered heads and turned to look at Johnny, Ruairi, and Mae Robin approaching.

But they weren’t greeted with the sad tears they were expecting as they finally made it to their friends. Breathless and worried, they noticed everyone had tears in their eyes and smiles on their faces. A little brown head slowly popped up from the coat in Lily-May’s lap.

A shaking but smiling Finn Hare.

Chapter 8
Mad as a March hare

Gleeful chatter across the glade could be heard for miles around that afternoon as they gathered around the fire. The joy in their voices could almost be bottled, such was its power.

Lily-May was a hero. Everyone smiled warmly towards her with admiration for her strength.

"I didn't do it all," she insisted as the others filled in Johnny, Ruairi, and Mae Robin on the events of earlier. "Finn would not be here with us if not for every single one of you, especially you Pádraig. We all had a part to play."

"But it sounds like your quick thinking was the root of such a brave story, Lily-May," Ruairi stated proudly, his warm furry body sitting against Lily-May's back to help keep her warm. "You should be beyond proud of yourself for preventing what could have been a huge tragedy."

“We will forever be grateful to you, young Lily-May,” Eostre, Finn’s mother, said sincerely. “You saved my only son, and I will never forget it.”

Lily-May smiled as she continued to gently rub Finn’s body in the coat on her lap even though she was beginning to get cold. She didn’t mind though. She loved Finn, and holding onto his weary body gave her comfort.

“Now,” Eostre the wise old hare continued, her voice firming up, “might I ask what my wonderful son was doing in the middle of the frozen lake anyways?” She stared deep into the eyes of her still shivering son Finn Hare.

“Eh yes, actually,” Fiadh Fawn commented with her normal, even, well-spoken tone back in her voice. “What on Earth were you doing?”

“Ehhhh, boxing,” Finn replied sheepishly, his small cheeks flushing.

“Boxing?” Lily-May asked. She wasn’t expecting him to say that!

"Well, practising," Finn corrected, his voice a little louder. "The annual contest is happening tomorrow, and I got completely caught up in my training. I lost my sense of direction! I didn't realise I'd gone out onto the ice until I heard the crack, and then, next thing I knew, I was gone under. It was freezing!"

"Well, obviously it was freezing, you nincompoop!" Eostre quickly remarked. "That was so silly of you, Finn. You nearly died."

"I know, I know," he said with his head lowered. "I'm really sorry."

"Wait! What annual contest?" Lily-May asked curiously.

"Every year, the male hares across the land come together to box," Ruairi explained, "to see who the strongest and most dominant male in the group is. The winner gets the honour of choosing his mate for the coming year. Assuming he's impressed her, of course."

"Ohhh," Lily-May grinned. She looked down at Finn, who gave her a cheeky wink.

"See, as mad as a march hare sis! Anyways, thankfully it all worked out in the end," Johnny blurted out, the biggest smile on his face as he walked over to Lily-May and Finn and rubbed both their heads. "Now it just so happens you've found who you were looking for sis, not just one but four! So go on, ask your question!" he ushered.

"Johnny! Now is hardly the time," Lily-May sniped back as she flashed her brother an embarrassed glance.

"There's no time like the present," Johnny answered quickly. He was just as keen as she was to find out the truth. "Ask!"

"Ask what?" Eostre enquired, clearly gathering that they, herself, Finn and her two daughters, Arleigh and Amaris, were the 'four' Johnny had referred to.

Lily-May let out a long sigh and cut Johnny a look that could kill. She took a deep breath and almost apologetically looked at Eostre and the hares one by one.

"My grandad has been telling me stories, old stories," she began, her voice slow and unsure.

"Very good," Eostre said with a hint of knowing where this conversation was going. "And?"

"Well, one of them is about the great warrior Oísin and the day he vowed never to hunt a hare again," Lily-May's voice trailed off as she looked to the ground embarrassed.

"I see," Eostre said in a firm, unemotional voice. She shot Ruairi a glance, and he nodded slightly.

"So, do you want to know about us shapeshifting?" Eostre asked directly.

Lily-May and Johnny's heads popped up as they leaned forward with their hearts skipping a beat.

"Yes!" they eagerly answered in unison.

"That's not something we talk openly about here," Eostre replied.

Their heads dropped down again, and their bodies slumped back. Both of their hearts sank.

"But," Eostre continued slowly as if weighing up the thoughts of her words, "considering I am now in my debt to you..."

Wordlessly, she tapped her foot repeatedly against the earth as she mulled over how best to proceed. The thumping of her foot mimicked Lily-May and Johnny's heartbeats as they skipped in anticipation.

"Finn, are you ok to walk?" the wise old hare asked her son.

"Em, yes. I think so," he answered, stretching out his long, firm body under the coat on Lily-May's lap.

"Very good. Girls, please ensure this fire is put out correctly and help your brother get back on his feet," Eostre gestured to her two daughters. "It's time young Johnny and Lily-May came for a walk with me."

Eostre elegantly stood up and turned her body away from the group towards the forest at the other side of the glade. She looked over her shoulder at the children with her wise deep-brown eyes and gestured for them to follow her. She slowly began to walk, her body low to the ground, ears flat along her back.

Johnny leapt to his feet like there was a spring underneath him and awkwardly caught up with Eostre, nearly tripping over a scrog of grass with haste. He grinned wildly at Ruairi, giving him an over-enthusiastic thumbs up.

Lily-May nearly threw Finn off her lap with excitement to get up and follow his mother! But she gathered herself quickly and instead gently placed Finn on his feet as she stood up. Her legs were a little stiff from sitting for so long, but that would not stop her now.

She looked at Ruairi, who gave her a small smile and a nod.

"Coming," she cried excitedly as she ran the couple of steps to catch up with her brother and the mysterious old hare.

Chapter 9

As quiet as a mouse

"I still can't believe it," Johnny was murmuring as he and his sister emerged from the enchanted rabbit tunnel back into their garden.

It was nearly seven o'clock in the evening. The sky was peppered with shades of red and purple blurring together as the last rays of sunlight illuminated the world above them. Both siblings' tummies began rumbling with hunger as they walked towards the back door. Ruairi trotted along beside them.

He didn't speak now he was back in the human world. Out of the Magical Wild, he reverted to the simpler life of a large cute fluffy brown and black dog who loved snuggles and belly rubs just as much as the next dog. Johnny wouldn't dare rub Ruairi's tummy in the Magical Wild or throw a stick for him to fetch. Ruairi would be less than impressed!

Lily-May beamed ecstatically, a million thoughts flying around her head as she ran for the back door. Her bag felt heavy on her back with the weight of the soggy coat, still ever so slightly warm from drying the thick fur of Finn Hare. She was cold without it, but that didn't matter. She'd found out the truth.

Eostre told them exactly what happens each full moon and even pointed out sacred areas in the Wild. Lily-May knew she should have been satisfied with this. She had heard it straight from the mouth of the most enchanted creature after all. But she felt a niggle. Sometimes, some things just must be seen to be believed.

Lily-May had formed a plan by the time her hand pushed down the handle on the backdoor to their house. The stove's heat hit her like a warm blanket as she entered the kitchen. She met Grandad's gaze, but all he got from her was a curious smile as she sped past him towards the hall door.

"Tell me!" Grandad shouted in astonishment when he realised she would not stop to talk.

"Later, Grandad," she answered back over her shoulder. "I've gotta have a shower and warm myself up first."

And then she vanished through the door into the hall.

Suddenly, Johnny burst through the backdoor and shouted excitedly for Grandad, “You *won’t* believe this old man!”

“Oi!” Grandad exclaimed, “less of the ‘old man’!”

Johnny grinned as he threw on the warm tap to wash his mud-stained hands at the kitchen sink.

“Stick on the kettle,” he gestured to his Grandad. “It’s time I tell *you* a story, Grandad Magory!”

He dried his hands on the tea towel and took a seat at the kitchen table, barely able to contain himself with excitement. Grandad clapped his hands together, rubbing them rigorously as he leapt up to the kettle, grinning like a young child.

* * *

Later that evening, Lily-May yawned as she stretched herself out on the three-seater couch. She snuggled up on Da’s chest with her grandmother’s old patchwork crocheted blanket draped over the two of them. With her feet on Ma’s lap, she quickly announced, “I’m off to bed.”

"This early?" her Da questioned her suspiciously. "Sure, the movie isn't even over yet?"

"Been a looonnng day, Da," she answered as she stood and did a wildly exaggerated yawn.

"So, I heard," he agreed before leaning across and kissing her on the cheek.

"Night mó stór," Ma said, leaning to kiss her other cheek.

"Good night, *hero*!" Johnny sneered as he took a fist-full of popcorn and shoved it into his gob.

"Tell Grandad I said 'goodnight' when he gets home from the pub," Lily-May said. She playfully kicked her brother's shoulder as he lay on the giant orange beanbag he'd gotten from Santa that Christmas. As she walked towards the hall door, Ruairi was curled up on the ground dozing in front of the blazing turf fire.

Lily-May was quite tired after today's drama, but she had no intention of going to sleep. Not after everything she'd learned earlier from Eostre, the wise old hare. In its true form like this, Magic was not only rare nowadays, but it was also practically unheard of. In just over an hour, something transformational was going to happen in the Wild, and she was not going to miss it.

No. Lily-May would sneak out when the grandfather clock in the hall struck nine bells.

It was just half eight now. Time enough for her to brush her teeth, silently pack her bag and 'pretend' to go to sleep.

When she had prepared, she crawled into her single bed and tried to take deep breaths to relax, but they didn't work. She picked up a book and tried to read, but she couldn't concentrate.

In the end, she closed her eyes and practised taking slow deep breaths and counting to four each time she inhaled and exhaled.

She glanced at her watch. Eight fifty-eight glowed back at her. It was time. She silently slipped out of bed and stuffed her pillow and teddy bears under the duvet to give the impression of her body. She quietly threw her packed bag onto her back and picked up her warm wellies beside the radiator.

Holding her breath, she opened her bedroom door just wide enough for her to slip out and pulled it closed behind her. Tiptoeing across the landing towards the stairs, she could hear the muffled music of the RTÉ nine o'clock news coming through the closed door of the sitting room downstairs. The grandfather clock in the hall clanged its first bell. DONG!

Tiptoeing down the steps, carefully avoiding the squeaky, creaky areas she knew by heart, she reached the bottom of the stairs. Turning towards the front door, she could hear Johnny tell his parents that he was "going to hit the hay."

As the ninth bell rang, she quickly and silently ran towards the front door without hesitating. Then, gently twisting the unlocked handle that had been left that way for Grandad to return from the pub, Lily-May slipped out into the freezing, starry night before her brother even opened the sitting-room door.

She tiptoed to the side gate of the house, ducking underneath the sitting room window. When she was in the darkness of the tight alleyway that led between her house and her neighbours, she unzipped her bag.

She took out her hat with the headtorch, her other brown coat, and gloves. She put everything on, zipping the coat right up to her chin. With the headtorch firmly on over her woolly hat, she zipped and closed her bag and put it on her back as she ran towards the enchanted rabbit hole at the back of the garden.

Lily-May bent down to enter it, a smile parting her lips.

She had done it, snuck out like a ninja or a spy in the movies.

As quiet as a mouse.

She was about the see the unbelievable.

And nobody had seen her.

Or so she thought.

Chapter 10
See it to believe

"Something told me I'd see you again tonight," a mysterious voice whispered from the dark just as Lily-May approached the clearing at the other side of the forest.

From the long grasses, Eostre emerged. Her brown coat glistened under the frost and light of the moon. Her deep dark eyes twinkled.

Lily-May smiled an embarrassed smile. Did Eostre think her obsession with them was rude? Did she think she was just a nosey little girl who asked too many questions for her own good?

Lily-May liked Eostre, but something about her made her feel uneasy. It was like Eostre held and guarded more wisdom than anyone she had ever met. Even Ruairi.

"You have a right to know, child. Don't fear," Eostre said. "Come with me."

"What do you mean 'a right to know'?'" Lily-May questioned cautiously. Ruairi had told her that she and Johnny descended from an ancient bloodline before but he refused to elaborate on it.

"The universe has a magical way of unfolding child. It will only reveal it's secrets to you at the right moment. And you'll find, that only at that moment, you will be ready to understand what it's sharing," Eostre answered wisely as they walked through the frozen scrogs of grass toward the centre of the glade.

Lily-May soaked up the beauty of the wild at night as they walked in silence. The perfectly formed cobwebs were visible in the glistening frost. The gently bobbing frozen heads of the rushes silhouetted against the glorious blueish white moon.

"You will take my place tonight, child," Eostre said calmly.

Lily-May held her breath. Had she heard correctly?

"I must sit with Finn tonight. He's still not right."

She exhaled loudly. Her shoulders steadily rose up and down from her ears as she tried to calm herself with slow deep breaths.

A short walk later, they emerged onto the centre of the glade, where the grass was low and flat. Arleigh and Amaris sat side by side on the cold grass, their backs straight as their heads were tilted upward towards the glowing full moon. It was almost like they were in a trance. They never turned to look at Eostre or Lily-May.

“I don’t know what to do?” Lily-May said to Eostre, a nervous twinge in her voice.

“Don’t worry, child. It’s inside you. You’ll know.”

Arleigh and Amaris slowly stood up on their hind legs and smiled a warm smile at Lily-May. Their eyes still seemed lit as if in a trance. They slowly walk towards her on their hind legs as though they had been expecting her. Standing upright like this, their elegant heads were at Lily-May’s shoulder, and she could feel the warmth of their fur as they got nearer.

Amaris stood to her left and Arleigh to her right. They placed their gentle paws in Lily-May’s hands which reassured her and filled her with a warm fuzzy feeling. They continued to step out until they formed a circle between the three of them. Eostre stood in the centre of the circle, smiling.

The sound of flutes could suddenly be heard from seemingly nowhere, as though carried on the gentle wind. It was a happy but slow, almost haunting kind of melody.

"Dance, my children," Eostre whispered from the centre of the circle.

Arleigh and Amaris standing on their hind legs, gracefully began to sidestep to the right, smiling and gesturing to Lily-May to do the same. A ripple of giddiness moved through the trio as they crossed their left legs behind the right, grinning broadly.

The magic music got louder, and the tempo began to increase slightly. The glistening frost reminded Lily-May of glitter on a dancefloor, and the moon reminded her of a disco ball that made everything in sight twinkle magically. Lily-May began to hop and swing her arms by her side, encouraged by the smiles of the three hares.

The music got faster again. The dancing trio continued to move in a circle in a clockwise direction, hopping, jumping, waving their arms in the air above their heads and laughing. Lily-May could feel the energy pulsing through every inch of her body, a mix of excitement and an indescribable connection to the hares. She felt her skin tingling, almost like the feeling of pins and needles. She could hear no other sound other than the sweet melody of the flutes and the shrill giggles of the hares.

Faster and faster they danced, laughing, cheering, and singing. They moved quickly as Lily-May's hands joined the paws of the hares on either side of her.

Eostre had disappeared from the centre of the circle. The trio whooped, cheered, jumped, and danced rejoicefully under the giant bright moon.

With her head swaying rhythmically, blurry, dizzy scenes of the tight circle filled her eyes. Lily-May let go of all control. She was having a ball with the hares and the music. She felt like she was in a trance.

Faster and faster.

She didn't notice for a while that the music began to slow. Only when she was nearly back at a walking pace did she realise.

Smiling wildly, she looked at the beaming faces of Arleigh and Amaris. She felt like she had left her body for a few minutes, but the pins and needles feeling was starting to fade, and she could feel herself returning. She wiggled her toes, tensed the muscles in her legs, and swayed her hips from side to side. She felt great, so alive.

Wanting to saviour the memory of this magic dance, she closed her eyes tightly and forced her brain to saviour everything about this moment. She was mindful of the energy buzzing through her body, the smell of the frost and the hares, the touch of their warm breaths against her cold cheek, and the sound of their panting and giggles. Once she was sure she had captured everything, she slowly opened her eyes to look at the moon once more before lowering them towards the warm fuzzy paws of the hares.

It was then she noticed.

There was no longer a pair of human hands and two pairs of hare paws in their tight circle, but rather three pairs of hare paws, each holding onto each other.

Chapter 11
Magic at work

A shrill, terrified scream escaped Lily-May's lips, and she pulled her arms back to her body, shaking them as she let go of the hares' paws. She was no longer human.

Although she knew this could happen from her talk with Eostre earlier, she had expected the hares to shapeshift to humans, not the other way around. How would she turn back? What would her Grandad say when he found out she had *actually* shapeshifted?

Excitement soon began to seep in, and it didn't take long for the intoxicating joy to fill her.

"I'm a hare," she screamed wildly and suddenly stopped, clasping a hand over her mouth at the sound that came out of her. Squeaky and high-pitched, she sounded like she had just sipped helium from a balloon! This only made her more excited, and she laughed as her new hare sisters hugged her tightly, all overcome with joy.

Embracing her and holding her two paws in her own, Eostre looked deep into Lily-May's eyes.

Lily-May could see the whole universe in the old hare's eyes. She was blessed with the knowledge of thousands of years and was overcome with respect and awe for the wisdom that Eostre possessed.

"I thought you'd prefer it this way, child," Eostre smiled sincerely. "It's not every day we get a new member to run as one of us. Now, you know what to do, Lily-May. We oversee the reawakening of the earthly wild magic. Have fun but remember why you're here."

Lily-May was so overjoyed she just nodded enthusiastically.

"Wanna give those legs a try?" Amaris grinned at her sister and put her four paws on the frozen earth. "It'll be just a little faster than what you're used to," she said with a wink before exploding into a gallop towards the forest at the edge of the glade.

"Come on," Arleigh shouted as she too put her four paws on the ground and erupted into a blurry sprint.

Lily-May was bewildered for just a moment, unsure how to instruct her now four legs to move like her hare sisters, but instinct kicked in. It was almost like she had done this before. Stretching out her long, strong body and propelling herself from her powerful hind legs, she erupted swiftly and elegantly into a gallop.

"Stay safe," Eostre smiled after the three hares.

"This is amazing!" Lily-May shouted as she flew along the cool, glistening grass. Her four paws moved in unison as she ran to catch her sisters.

They sat waiting for her at the edge of the thick sleeping forest.

"Not bad for a newbie," Amaris grinned when Lily-May joined them.

"She's not really a newbie," Arleigh winked. "Anyways, we've got work to do, ladies."

Arleigh was older than Amaris and Finn and was very responsible compared to her siblings.

"Lily-May, you come with me for the first while, and I'll show you the ropes. Then you can go on your own."

Lily-May nodded in agreement, catching her newfound furry ears lopping from the corner of her deep brown eyes.

"Remember to meet back here at sunrise," Arleigh shouted at her younger sister, who had already taken off eastwards.

"Of course," Amaris shouted as she galloped into the distance. "Have fun you two!"

A row of enormous oak trees spread out before them like a wall separating the glade from the rest of the world as the two hares slowly walked side by side in the moonlight.

"Intent is more powerful than words, Lily-May," Arleigh began as she sat at the base of one of the ancient trees and stared lovingly at the bare trunk.

"Once we are thinking loving thoughts, love will flow from us into whatever we are focusing on," she continued, not moving her eyes from the trunk of the tree.

"And in turn, that object of our attention, no matter what it is, will return that loving energy to us in gratitude.

"But words are important. The ancients love their words," she said as she closed her eyes and mysteriously whispered, "Dúisigh agus fás. Draíocht fiáin."

Arleigh raised her right paw and placed it on the wrinkled bark as Lily-May stared without moving. Arleigh repeated the sentence three times with her eyes firmly closed, deep in concentration and dedication. Her words were crystal clear, almost as vivid as the deep pools of her eyes as she opened them again and smiled at Lily-May.

"Now we need to do this to everything that still lies sleeping," she explained to Lily-May. "We've got different rituals depending on the time of year, but for now, with the Spring Equinox and full moon, it's all about making sure everything hears us say '*awaken and grow, wild magic*' in our native tongue."

"Everything?" Lily-May questioned a little hesitantly. After all, everything would mean every tree, shrub, blade of grass. She was certainly excited about her job, but it didn't take a genius to realise it would take three of them a thousand years to carry out this ritual to every single thing in the Wild!

Arleigh chucked as she stooped down to pick up some rubbish at the base of the oak tree.

"No, not everything!" she answered. "I've just spoken with this oak. She will instruct her fellow sisters now that I've awoken her, but the hawthorns need to be spoken to separately, as do the birch, the hedgehogs, the frogs and all the other sleeping groups."

"Phew!" Lily-May was, relieved. This made the job a lot more attainable.

"Remember to pick up any rubbish you see, Lily-May," Arleigh instructed as she unearthed another plastic wrapper from under a patch of frozen grass and placed it in plain view. "The badgers will gather it up for us and dispose of it properly, but it's important we remove as much as we can at this time of year before all the little critters are born in the coming months."

"Of course," Lily-May answered, her heart heavy at the sight of human waste in the beautiful Wild.

"Great. Ok, Amaris is gone for the mountains. I will look after the lake, the glade, and the edge of the forest tonight if you can go into the forest and make your way back towards your home. Ok?"

"Yes, boss," Lily-May grinned. This is so cool! See you soon," and with that, she took off towards the path she knew so well back through the deep forest to play with her newfound magic.

Chapter 12
Follow your nose

The night sky enveloped Lily-May, as the moon cascaded shadows around her with the Wild in plain sight before her. No need for a torch when you are a hare, she thought. Her eyesight was far better than her human eyes. She could see perfectly in the dark. She could hear things she had never heard before, like worms slowly moving underground beneath her. She pricked her ears in delight when she listened to the slow dripping heartbeat of the trees. Turning her head slightly, she heard rustling leaves in the distance that she knew was Arleigh moving away from her. She could smell things she never knew existed. The scent of the frost was strong, as were the aromas of her different friends in the wild. She could feel things too, like a blade of grass brushing against the long whiskers on her nose. But the most incredible sense she had now was the internal voices of all her animal friends nearby. Being able to communicate without talking or body language felt terrific to her. It was like she was seeing, hearing, feeling, smelling, and embracing the world for the very first time. She wondered what grass would taste like but decided there were certain things she could do with not knowing about!

Lily-May sat at the foot of a familiar huge Scots Pine and slowly and precisely placed the five fluffy toes of her front right paw onto the deeply riveted, cold bark. She looked at the tree as though she had never looked at it before. She felt so much love for the tree, and slowly but surely, she could feel the tree sending the love back to her through her outstretched paw. She was in such a state of peace and love that she could almost see wisps of energy move between them. She closed her eyes and said to the tree, "Dúisigh agus fás. Draíocht fiáin." (*Awaken and grow, wild magic)*

Sparks of electricity passed through them both as the tree listened and began to slowly wake and send messages to the others.

"This is incredible," Lily-May said aloud as she moved on to her next job, a giant Mountain Ash.

She repeated her job diligently as she went back through the forest towards the Golden River and Master Willow.

She worked with both of them, although Master Willow would not stop singing to her! This made it a little harder to concentrate, and Lily-May questioned whether she had to do the job for him, considering just how awake he always was!

Rubbish dotted throughout the beautiful wild saddened Lily-May. As a human, she would always pick up litter when she saw it. But now, as an animal, she was astonished by the sheer amount of it that she would never have noticed through human eyes. It wasn't easy for her hare body to pull out crisp packets the grass had grown over in the last season or to untangle disposable face masks wrapped around twigs and branches. But she did, and she was determined not to let it get her down during her work. She could worry about it later.

As Lily-May moved closer towards the magic rabbit hole that led back into her garden, she picked up a faint scent. It felt familiar to her hare brain but not her human one.

She followed the scent which went westwards along the hedgerow of hawthorn and blackthorn. The ditch below the hedge was dried out and filled with dead leaves that crunched underneath her paws as she slowly walked. She occasionally stopped to work on the various shrubs and trees as she followed the scent.

It grew stronger, and Lily-May hopped excitedly from the joy of this new game of following her nose. Slowly she stepped on the frozen leaves under the hedgerow inching forward to the smell, which was so strong now she felt like she could touch it.

With her nose low to the ground, she moved another inch.

"Ouch!" she yelled suddenly as a sharp prick stuck into the tip of her soft black nose.

"Ouch!" she yelled again as she rubbed her soft furry paw off her nose and noticed a drop of blood.

"What on earth is that?" Lily-May said aloud as she carefully used her paws to move some of the frozen leaves that lay on the ground where she had pricked her nose.

"Grainne," she said quietly with a smile from ear to ear as she realised who the curled up, sleeping hedgehog nestled in the leaves was.

Lily-May loved Grainne and her family and missed them dearly every winter when they disappeared to hibernate.

She was so proud to get to work waking up her prickly friend and did the best job she could.

"Dúisigh agus fás. Draíocht fiáin."

Just as she was finishing, she thought she caught the scent of something else but quickly forgot when her little friend slowly blinked her eyes awake and began to uncurl and stretch her little body.

"Lily-May? Is that you?" squeaked the little hedgehog through a sleepy yawn.

"Yes, Grainne," Lily-May burst back with excitement. "Wow, I can't believe I got to help wake you up!"

She was hopping from one hind leg to the other with excitement, rubbing her front paws eagerly. A scent ran through her nostrils again, and her body sent a warning shiver. Unused to this instinctual feeling, she shrugged it off to enjoy the moment with Grainne.

"Me neither," said the slightly confused hedgehog as she rubbed her eyes. "I've clearly missed a lot this winter!"

Chapter 13

The chase of course

In a field, a short distance from Lily-May, stood two tall men wearing boots, long black coats, and black hats. At their side, held by a short chain, stood a powerful, agitated greyhound named Liath. One of the men had a large round lamp to scan the dark field that lay silent before them under the frost.

Liath was almost frenzied looking as he pulled aggressively at the short chain. His eyes were wild, showing the whites around them, and froth dripped from the sides of his long mouth.

The men were lamping and coursing for hares. Both are illegal activities in Ireland. They used the bright light from the lamp to stun unsuspecting animals such as hares, rabbits, and deer while releasing their greyhound to run it down and kill it. A cruel, disgusting, and unfair activity for any human to participate in.

The greyhound had not been fed or walked for days which left him feeling crazy. The men had done this on purpose.

Silently they stood, shining the lamp across the field along the hedgerows. A slight movement in the distance caught all their attention, and they each recognised the long, slender ears of a hare at that moment. The men's pulses began to race with the impending thrill of the chase. This energy seeped into Liath, who was ravenous with hunger. Not a word was uttered as one of the men stooped down and unclicked the chain that held the dog. The other held the lamp deadly still on the target.

The dog erupted from their side in a wild gallop, stretching his long, lean body to the limits as he hit speeds of nearly seventy kilometres an hour within seconds.

His lean muscular body cast a giant shadow across the frozen field as he raced away from the lamp and towards the stunned hare.

It only took him four seconds to reach the hedgerow where the terrified hare sat, eyes wide with fear. Froth fell from Liath's exposed teeth as he took one final jump to land and catch his prey. Ending his starvation was his only thought.

Chapter 14
Sett you free

Lily-May could not move. Her body simply refused to. Her mind screamed at her to move, to run, to use her sleek hare body and escape the terrifying, frothing jaws that were now mere centimetres from her face. But she could not move. It was like fear had frozen her to the spot just as the frost had frozen the dead leaves under the hedgerow of hawthorns.

The only thing she could do was shut her eyes and pray. So, she did.

The force of another creature crashed into the paralysed hare, brutally crushing her into the ground. Closing her eyes tighter, she braced her frozen body.

The other creature kept pushing her to the ground.

'This is it,' Lily-May thought to herself. She was even too afraid to cry.

"Move, child," a voice boomed. "Move, now, move."

Lily-May recognised the voice. It was Ruairi. She opened her eyes, but everything was dark.

"Ruairi?"

"Run, Lily-May! Get your feet underneath you and run, child."

"Where are we?"

"In the badger's sett, and I can't go any further with you. It's too tight, so you must run, now. I'll block them from you."

It was like a switch clicked inside Lily-May's head. The fear that had frozen her sat aside for a moment letting her body and mind work together once more. She put her paws underneath her and ran. She used her sense of touch and sound to guide her as she galloped blindly through the pitch-black tunnels.

Behind her, she could hear the ferocious sound of dogs fighting and men shouting. The snapping and snarling grew louder before wails of pain and yelping travelled across the field. Lily May ran faster, afraid to look back.

* * *

"This way Lily-May," she heard a familiar voice call, awakening her from the blind trance she had been in.

She had been running for what felt like hours, not knowing where she was going or how far she had travelled. It was Brocleigh Badger, and she knew by the depth of voice as it reverberated off the tight earthy tunnel that he was about three metres up ahead. She stopped suddenly to get her bearings as a soft paw reached out and touched her.

"It's ok," he reassured her. "Follow me."

As they crossed into the earthy tunnel, the sound of their padding paws echoed through the earth while Lily-May's heartbeat thumped heavily. She was safe.

Chapter 15

Cut the rubbish

"Thank the Spirits you followed her," Eostre Hare said as she worked on Ruairi's wounds under the glare of the full moon. "Nobody could have foreseen that Ruairi. Disgusting humans."

"Hmmm," Ruairi simply replied as he tried to mask the pain of the bite marks on his legs from the greyhound and the bruising on his ribcage from the boots of the two men.

"She's safe, Ruairi," a hauting, shrill voice suddenly called from above.

A ghostly figure flew above their heads to deliver the good news. Luna Barn Owl perched silently on a bare branch of the old oak tree that shaded Eostre and Ruairi from the chilly wind.

"Brocleigh Badger found her," Luna said. "They've left the sett north of the Golden River. She's totally unharmed, and they're making their way here now," she informed them.

“Drink this,” Eostre said, placing a little wooden bowl with a strange, whitish glowing liquid in it in front of him.

Ruairi knew Eostre longer than anybody else. He knew that he trusted her with every fibre of his being, so he bent down to the bowl and drank without questioning.

“Ahhhh,” he said in relief when he had finished the last drop and licked his lips.

He could feel a healing warmth rush through his body. Eostre patted herbs and liquid onto his open wounds, and Ruairi watched in amazement as the cuts began to heal before his eyes.

“Thank you, old friend,” he smiled at the hare. “And thank you, Luna, for the update. It looks like I’ll be right as rain before Lily-May arrives, so neither of you are to breathe a word to her about my wounds. She does not need to worry about this. The less she knows, the better.”

* * *

Sprinting along the bank of the Golden River, Lily-May and Brocleigh made their way to the glade in the hope of finding their friends safe. They both knew from the position of the moon that dawn would be upon them soon.

"I'm so glad Luna Barn Owl was able to let me know Ruairi is ok," Lily-May said to Brocleigh.

"Yes, we're pretty good at spreading the word fast out here in the Wild," Brocleigh Badger agreed.

The badger panted heavily with the pace of the hare, even though he knew she could go much faster as each step took them closer to the glade.

When they reached the edge of the forest, they could see figures in the middle of the clearing. Lily-May's heart nearly burst as she noticed Ruairi's silhouette, sitting up nobly as he always did out here with the shape of Eostre Hare beside him. Racing towards him as fast as her four paws could carry her, she tore away from Brocleigh with the happiest of smiles on her cute furry face.

"Thank the Spirits, he's ok," Lily-May felt relieved. "I would never forgive myself if anything happened to him."

"You don't need to worry about our King Lily-May. Ruairi is the best fighter anyone here has ever known," Brocleigh said with admiration. "Not that he ever really fights often," he added hastily, "and I'm fairly sure he's the one that needs to worry about you and your brother Johnny more than you two will ever have to worry about him!"

"Maybe," Lily-May said, but she was distracted, having noticed the piles of rubbish stacked throughout the glade. Plastic sweet and crisp wrappers, disposable face masks, empty glass bottles.

"Brocleigh, I can't believe how much rubbish is piled up out here," she said with a heavy heart.

"Yeah, it's pretty bad," Brocleigh admitted, "and it seems to be getting worse each year. It's like all those humans don't give a damn about the world. They've no idea the harm they cause to us, regardless of the age but the young ones especially."

"I give a damn," Lily-May said quietly to herself, embarrassed at her human race, "I would never dream of hurting anything out here."

"Ooouuuccccchhh!" she cried suddenly as she fell over into the long grass.

"Lily-May, what's wrong?" Brocleigh said in confusion.

"My leg," she sobbed. "I'm after catching the back of my leg on something Brocleigh."

"It's a sharp crushed metal tin that was stuck on that scrog of grass," Brocleigh pointed back. "Are you ok?"

"Yes, I'll be fine," she sobbed again as blood trickled down her long muscular hind leg.

She limped slowly towards Ruairi and Eostre as she realised how tired she was. Her legs were weary, and her eyes felt heavy. It had been a long night, but she forgot it all when she wrapped her paws around Ruairi and nestled into the thick, brown fur on his chest.

"Thank you, Ruairi," she whispered, tears flowing down her face. "I'm so sorry I got you into that fight. I hope they didn't hurt you."

"I'm fine, child," he replied in a deep, sincere voice. "I'm just grateful I was in the right place at the right time."

"Were you following me?" Lily-May asked slightly indignantly. Yes, she knew she'd very nearly been killed, but she was capable of looking after herself.

"It's a lucky thing I heard you tiptoe down the stairs earlier tonight, young lady," Ruairi replied with the air of a parent disciplining their child.

Lily-May knew he was right, so she just lowered her head and snuggled in tighter to his warm chest. She didn't say a word more.

Arleigh and Amaris bounded across the clearing shortly after towards their mother.

"All done," they shouted in unison, skidding to a halt and exhaling a satisfied breath.

"Eh, did we miss something?" Amaris said, gesturing to Ruairi and Lily-May.

Lily-May was curled up in a ball at Ruairi's feet, barely awake. She smiled at the three hares in front of her and shut her eyes. Exhaustion had taken control of her body, and she did not resist.

Chapter 16
Tell me a story

"Wake up, Lily-May," Johnny was calling to his sister from the bottom of her bed. "Come on, the hare boxing championships are gonna kick off soon, and I'll go without you if you don't get up!"

Lily-May slowly blinked her eyes open. The bright blue sky and the morning sun shone through the frosted bedroom window.

"You'd swear you'd been up all night," Johnny moaned as his impatience grew. "Come on. You've still to get breakfast."

"Ok, ok," she answered groggily. "What time is it?"

"Half eleven," Johnny replied exasperated. "I've been calling you since nine lazy bones!"

Lily-May tried to lift her head off the pillow but only managed to raise it a small bit before collapsing back. She felt exhausted.

"Are you sick or what?" her brother demanded, "cause you're not ruining my day. I've been waiting all year for this!"

"Jeez, thanks Johnny," she groaned. "No, I'm not sick, just really tired."

"Why?" Johnny asked.

Ruairi padded through the bedroom door, jumped onto Lily-May's bed and gave her face a big lick. At that moment, visions began flashing before Lily-May's eyes. Hares, full moons, hunters. Was it all a dream?

She pulled off the duvet cover and saw she was in her pyjamas. Her heart sank. It must have been a dream. She must have fallen asleep before the clock struck nine.

The images in her head were getting clearer and clearer, though. The glowing full moon. The pristine visions of the frozen wild. She had never seen it that clearly before. These images were different. Confusion flashed all over her pale face.

"What's the matter?" Johnny asked, noticing his sister's expression change. "You look like you've seen a ghost."

"I..." Lily-May began, but her heart was too sad to continue. How wonderful it had all been. She wished it had been true as the images of Brocleigh Badger, Grainne Hedgehog and Luna Barn Owl all crystalised in her mind.

"What?" Johnny pushed.

"I..." she began again, "had the most wonderful dream. But I wish it were true."

She crashed her head back onto the pillow again, pulling the duvet up to hide her teary eyes. She wished more than anything that it could have been real.

Yawning and showing all his teeth, Ruairi shuffled on the bed, trying to get comfortable. He moved awkwardly over the lumps and bumps with his giant paws until he found the right spot and slumped down heavily on Lily-May's legs.

"Ow, Ruairi," she shouted as she leapt up in the bed. "My leg!"

And then she remembered.

She whipped off the duvet covers so fast that they fell onto the floor.

Sitting up straight, Lily-May pushed Ruairi aside and pulled up the leg of her pyjama bottom on her right leg.

Johnny gasped. "Ouch, that looks sore," he said, staring at a long cut on the outside of his sister's thigh.

The thin deep cut curved in a line from the top of her thigh to just above her knee. Dried blood smeared along the wound.

Lily-May's eyes widened.

Her heart quickened.

She stared at Ruairi, who simply winked back.

"Grandad!" she shouted. Excitement oozed off her voice. "Quick, Grandad!"

Grandad bounded up the stairs in fright, not knowing what was wrong with his granddaughter.

He burst through the door adjacent to the bed and stopped next to Johnny. Deep furrowed wrinkles stretched across his forehead as his chest heaved after sprinting up the stairs. Eyes wide, both Johnny and Grandad looked entirely confused.

"Have I got a story for *you*..." she beamed.

The End

The truth about shapeshifters

Hi reader, I hope you liked this scéal. I really enjoyed writing this, especially the research I had to do. In Ireland we have so much amazing folklore documented throughout our history, it was hard to pull myself away from all the reading to actually write!

Firstly, let's just put it out there that I LOVE the wild hares of Ireland. They are my favourite native Irish mammal. I love their deep dark soulful eyes and their sleek powerful bodies. The fact that they can reach speeds of 50mph (80kph) over short distances leaves me in awe for such a small creature. Most of all though, I love those mysterious 'sídhe' (fairy) stories that surround them.

The story that Grandad tells at the start of this book is one of my favourite Irish legends, bet you would never have guessed! And as with all of our myths and legends, regardless of what country or continent you are on, I believe that there's no smoke without fire.

I think that our ancestors were far more in touch with the mystical side of life than we are today. But the growing popularity of humans reconnecting with nature might just lead to us all uncovering this kind of magic again soon.

I believe there's magic everywhere and that the shapeshifting of energy, which we are all made of, was and is possible. And in the meantime, a fun exercise I love to do is to mediate and visualise myself in different forms and locations.

Maybe you can try and quiet your mind the next time you are out in nature, I find trees really help.

Slán agus go raibh mile maith agat.

Emma-Jane

P.S - There's magic in the woods child, everyone knows it, but *you* need to remind them.

I'll tell you a story about Johnny McGory,
Will I begin it? That's all that's in it!